ISAIAH
40:3

That Damn Belt!

David W. Tuggle

PublishAmerica
Baltimore

First printing

All characters appearing in this work are fictitious. Any resemblance to real persons, living or dead, is purely coincidental.

ISBN: 1-4241-0128-X
PUBLISHED BY PUBLISHAMERICA, LLLP
www.publishamerica.com
Baltimore

Printed in the United States of America

For all those kids
With all those stories
Who simply want to be
…
Loved

Acknowledgements

I am thankful for so many people, but specifically a few folks without whom Danny's story would never have seen the light of day.

– Dad and Mom, who truly love me and always knew how to show it.

– Rebecca, Robert and Kevin, who continually support their older brother.

– David, Daniel, Sarah, Jon, and Jessie, for being the best friends I have ever had.

– That pizza server who told me once that I should just get off my butt and write the story…you know who you are.

– The entire launch team at New Hope North for the prayers and dedication you have given to serving and loving our Lord, Jesus Christ.

– Finally, thanks to my best friend, my Lord and Savior, Jesus Christ.

That room!

That belt!

That man…

I don't know what to do anymore.

I hate my life!

That Damn Belt!

I could kill him, I suppose, but then I'd probably just be in jail. But, how do I defend myself from him?

How can I make him stop?

Could I take him?

I'm 15.

He puts on such a happy front! All the neighbors, hell man, all the fuckin' city, think he walks on water. But then, every fuckin' night, every single fuckin' night, That Damn Belt! Just once I'd like to beat the living shit outta him…

I'm 15.

I could take him.

Yeah, that'll happen.

Maybe I can hide.

I used to think it was my fault, that I really was this horrible kid who deserved "discipline." I thought it was normal, what he did.

Normal?

Yeah.

Shit, man, if that's normal, I don't wanna be normal. If that's the way life is supposed to be, I don't wanna live here. I don't wanna live anywhere. If this is normal, normal sucks!

It's all so pointless. So stupid.

Should I tell someone? Who? No one would believe me.

Ashelee would believe me. It's nice having a girlfriend who cares and who listens and who trusts. In at least that way, I suppose, I'm lucky.

No one can help me.

Ashelee might help.

Could she?

No!

What am I supposed to say? *"Hi Sweetie! My dad beats the living shit outta me every single day. Can you fix it?"* She'd bail on me so quick, and I need her.

At least Ashelee loves me. Won't have sex, but she loves me.

I can't tell her.

Can't tell anyone.

What do I do?

I need someone to help…

At least I know that now, but so what?

Maybe I'll tell her dad, he's one of those church guys. A pastor or minister or something. I joke with him when I get over to her house and I call him "Pastor Dad."

No! I can't tell him. I can't tell nobody.

No one would ever believe it anyway, and then I'd just get it worse.

Shit!

What's worse than this? Can anything be worse than this?

That man's an ass and I'm supposed to call him "Dad"?

I'm 15 fuckin' years old and I can't take him…

There's not shit I can do. Nothing.

That Damn Belt!

The Trip...

One summer, the church took a group of kids on a week-long lakeside camping trip. The concept of "church camp" and spending a week with "church people" did not remotely appeal to me.

The concept of a week without the belt – that appealed to me.

No tiger.

No belt.

This was my second trip away from home. I only ever went away twice, once with my grandparents to their house for two weeks—seemed like heaven. Grandparents spoil! Two weeks without the belt Two weeks of playing with Gramps.

We'd go out in the yard and play catch. He loved to throw a ball, any ball! We used to go into their barn and talk with the animals. They didn't have too many, just a pig, which was the worst smell ever, two goats, and about 10 chickens, though I was never really sure how many chickens were running around. It was my job to pick up the eggs.

And then there was Fred. Fred was a cow, a mother cow. Not sure about naming a lady cow Fred, but Gramps was that way sometimes. I remember when Fred had a baby. I saw it come out. Calves are cool. I stuck my finger in its mouth and it sucked and sucked. Thought it was a nipple or something.

Grandpa liked to take me out to the edge of the property, by the river. There was an old cemetery there and he'd tell stories. I can still hear his voice.

"Dan-boy," he'd start, "this here stone marks the resting spot of your great-grandfather, Franklin Daniel. He was a man of God, a man who sought the Lord in everything he did. Dan-boy, I can see some of ol' Franklin in you. You have his hair and the flash of his eyes."

He talked about Great-Grandpa Franklin all the time.

I looked like him? I saw a picture once and I suppose we might look a little bit the same, but not that much.

Besides, I really didn't care. But, I listened.

"Dan-boy, one thing that Franklin had that you don't have is a smile. I don't remember the last time I saw a smile on your face. You know it takes more work to frown than to smile, Dan-boy, and you work awful hard!"

Gramps, I thought, if you only knew the man your daughter married, you'd get it then. Then you'd understand.

I loved the sound of Gramps's voice. He was so at peace. I don't know how else to say that. He was like peace, like no anger or hurt. Peace. I wish I coulda told him, but no. I couldn't tell anyone.

Being with Gramps and Grandma was a good time.

No pressure.

No pain.

Oh, and Grandma's cooking! Eating Grandma's cooking! She made the best damn fried chicken ever. If I close my eyes, I can still smell it. Fried chicken, mashed potatoes, gravy. Tons of gravy. Corn on the cob. Milk. Sometimes chocolate milk. Yum!

Breakfast! She loved cooking breakfast. We'd have eggs, bacon, sausage, hotcakes, grits or browned potatoes, and fresh orange juice. Yum!

When I close my eyes, it's almost like I'm there.

I can still smell Grandma. Her house. Her hair.

Peace.

Safety.

They took me to church. Twice. And they made me sit still and listen.

But, at the end of church, we had fried chicken and then we all went to the pond to go skating.

There's nothing like skating outside on a frozen pond.

I was ten then.

Now I was invited to church camp…away for another week.

Freedom?

No tiger.

No belt.

I was popular at school and there'd be tons of kids there. We'd be able to water ski and wake board and tube.

I always kept my shirt on in public. No one ever asked about it.

Didn't care?

Didn't know?

Didn't wanna know?

Ashelee would be there. It'd be fun and…I'd be safe for a time.

Free for a time.

The camp went great! We were up early for breakfast and a devotional time, then free time on the lake. Ashelee and I swam with the others, and

10

sailed. Sometimes the whole group would climb the hill, but some times she and I did it alone, too.

I remember the joy. Running through the sand, wind against our faces. The shirt never came off. The sweats always covered my legs. Ashelee never asked.

I think she knew, but she never asked. We swam. We laughed. We listened to her father talk about God. Pastor Dad always had a talk to give…he called it a message…and we always had to be there to listen. I guess that's part of church camp. He talked about a God who I'd never heard of. His messages were about a God who gave a rip.

How could any God give a rip about me?

No one did…except Ashelee. But then, she didn't know. A real God would know, I guess, but there wasn't any God. Right?

I listened, but I didn't believe it. Maybe I didn't want to.

All I knew was that I loved Ashelee. I loved being with Ashelee. I loved talking with Ashelee. I loved the thought of Ashelee.

I loved being away.

Free.

No tiger.

No belt.

On Thursday night, Ash's dad did a talk and invited people to accept Christ.

Accept Christ?

What did that mean?

"*He will forgive you,*" he said. "*Jesus loves you,*" he said. "*He will take care of you,*" he said.

Seemed fake to me, but Ashelee believed it all. Everything.

When he gave the call, people poured out and went running up to the front. Tons of them went. Nearly everyone.

I didn't get it. I didn't want to get it. I stayed.

Everybody moved.

Not me.

But, as I sat there watching, something happened that I'd never forget. Ashelee had gone up but, after a few minutes, she came back.

Back to me.

She just sat down right there, next to me, and held my hand.

"It's okay to question, Danny," she said. "It's okay not to understand. I don't always understand. I know Daddy doesn't understand everything, he just trusts Jesus. Faith, Danny."

Faith in what? I thought. I didn't get it. I didn't want to get it. But, still, there was something about Ashelee.

She didn't say anything else at first. She just sat there. But, then she started talking and she wasn't talking to me. She was talking to Someone else. Someone Who I didn't see.

"Hey, Jesus," she said. "Hold onto Danny, Jesus, and help him to see You and to feel You. Help Danny to know You, Jesus." And that was it. She stopped and we just sat there.

I didn't get it. What's the point of talking to the air? Even if there was a God, he sure wasn't gonna help me. Right?

But, Ashelee prayed. I didn't look at her, but I think she was crying.

I was thinking about the stuff Pastor Dad had said. I was thinking about my life. *My life really sucks*, I thought, *how can God really care or really understand. Where is He?*

After a while, Pastor Dad closed the night like he always did.

With prayer.

When everyone had filed out, heading down to the lake for evening games, Ashelee stayed.

We sat. Ashelee and I sat.

Pastor Dad came over. "You two take your time. Pray if you like. Danny, you know you can always talk with me," he said. "You can talk with me about anything you feel you need to vent or to talk about or to share. I just want you to know that." Ashelee squeezed my hand and her father continued, "Danny, you're 14 now and I want you to hear me say a few things."

Uh oh, I thought, *I have to be in trouble. What did I do? Is he like my father? All fathers are alike, right? Fuck, man, I knew it. I'm gonna get beat up by my girlfriend's dad, right in front of her.* I didn't know any better, but I did know that there was something different about this man. I just didn't get it.

Not then.

Not yet.

"First of all," he began, "I know you think you love Ashelee and, Danny, there is no one would rather have Ashelee spend time with."

Huh? I didn't believe what I was hearing. No one he'd rather have spend time with her. Fuck, man, didn't he know how evil I was?

He continued. "I know she loves you and I know she's been praying for you since you were both very little."

There's that word again—prayer.

"But, Danny, I want you to know that I pray for you, too. Our family prays for you and, Danny, we love you! We are here for you and we are your friends. I know you're a good kid and I believe that you and Ashelee are good for each other. You're good with each other. Good friends are key to growing up well. You two hang out as long as you like, but I don't think you'll want to miss too much of tonight's games...people will get very dirty before the night's over. S'mores over the fire, too!" Smiling and giving Ash a hug, he walked in the direction of the lake.

Did that man just tell me that they loved me? What does that mean?

My father, asshole, says he loves me.

This was different, though. Pastor Dad really seemed to care.

Ashelee and I sat there for a time before we headed down to join the others. Everyone was in and out of the water, swinging flaming marshmallows around on the end of sticks and having a great time. Ashelee and I joined in.

Friday ended the camp. We swam in the morning, right after breakfast and the morning devotional time, and then packed the vans to head home.

Home?

What is home supposed to be?

A place to sleep?

A place to dream?

A place to love?

A place with pain?

That Damn Belt!

The First Time…

I remember when it started…

"Can I go over to Jimmy's?" I know the answer before I even ask.

"Your father will want you to be here tonight, when he comes home."

It was always the same.

If I ever asked to do anything late in the afternoon, she always said the same thing. It was like a broken record or something. "You're father will want you to be here tonight, when he comes home."

I had to be there. I had to be in the house, doing homework, doing chores, doing anything.

And waiting. Waiting for him.

I don't know what it was that made me do it. It would be the same whether I was there or not. The belt was always there.

That Damn Belt!

I suppose for her that had to be it, cause maybe he'd hit her, too. Maybe he already did. Maybe he always had.

No, he wouldn't do that. Would he?

She wouldn't let him. Would she?

She'd leave then…right? If only. Fuck! If she'd had the balls to leave the first time…we'd be gone.

I remember the first time like it was yesterday. All the rest seem to blend in, but not the first time. I was little.

That Damn Belt!

Yeah, he'd hit me before, like the time I was just three. They gave me a big ol' truck for my birthday. Three fuck'n years old.

He comes home from work drunker than shit and screams at me to get off the floor and go to my room. I start to cry.

Mom looked at him and says, "Honey, it's his birthday present. He's just playing with the truck you gave him."

"Not down here, he's not! Not in my living room! He's in the way. He's in the fucking way all the fucking time!" he screamed, and kicked my truck clean outta my hands. "Hey! I told you to get the hell upstairs! GO!"

Up I went. And, when I get there…I start to play, that's all I'm doing. Playing.

Playing with my blocks.

He bursts in the door and screams at me to get on the bed. I start crying again and I guess I didn't move fast enough, cuz he picks me up and throws me on my bed.

He pulls my pants down.

I was three.

That Damn Belt!

Blood Lust...

He liked blood...my blood. Not sure why. He just liked to see my ass bleed.

I remember the first time I bled. I think I was 8.

He was pissed that night; I remember 'cause I was hiding in the day room, trying to do homework. I hate math. It was multiplication tables that night; I remember that 'cause of later.

He came in, not drunk this time, and exploded at me. "Why the hell did I trip over trash that you were supposed to take out?"

"Daddy, I had to do my homework. You told me I had to do my homework before I did anything."

"Don't give me any of your bullshit mouth! You left the damn trash in the kitchen. I never told you to do homework! Get upstairs! NOW!"

I panicked. I ran up the back stairs, but I didn't go to my room. I hid in the hall closet. Here would be safe, right? Not like the closet in my room.

He always looked in there first.

After what seemed like forever, he came up the front stairs and slammed the door to my room open.

I wasn't there.

He erupted in anger. "Where the fucking shit are you, you little bastard! You come out right now, or so help me..."

I was frozen.

His steps pounded on the old floors. He started down the hall. He walked by the closet. As I sat listening to him go by, I breathed a sigh.

He came back.

The closet door flew open. "You get into that damn room. Now!" His voice sounded like an explosion. "On your bed. And take off your clothes...all of them!"

I went into the room and slowly took my shirt off. Then my pants. Then my underwear. As I climbed onto the bed, I wet myself.

I wet everything.

I was so scared.

He came in and, making sure I could hear it, pulled his belt off. He started at the back of my knees and worked his way up. He made me count. When I got to eight, he turned the belt around and began with the buckle end. The buckle had a tiger head on it.

"You did your homework?" he bellowed. "Let's multiply eights. What's eight times two?"

"Si...si...sixteen!" I screamed.

"Good! How do you like the buckle?" he asked. He sounded like I always thought Satan would sound. "Look, blood!" he said. "That's good!"

Finally he stopped. But, he wasn't finished. From now on, he said, I was to come up here every day and, if I was lucky, I wouldn't need more.

"I am the father. I am in charge. You will remember that!"

I'll never forget that tiger.

Ever.

That Damn Belt!

Baseball...

I was 11. Does anyone get beat when they're 11? Maybe he'll quit now. Yeah right!

The baseball season was ready to start, I played third base and sometimes I got to pitch.

I liked pitching. Alone, out on the mound. All alone. No one could touch me...no one could hurt me. I was safe.

He came to the games.

Why did he have to come to the fuckin' games?

They were my games, right?

Why did he have to come to my fuckin' games?

He didn't give a shit; he just wanted me to know he was there.

Like I'd miss that.

I remember one day. One very bad day.

I started the game at third and was doing great. I'd made a double play on a line drive. I had two hits.

He wasn't there. Maybe he wasn't coming.

Maybe.

Two hits.

It was the sixth inning and there were runners on first and third. No outs.

Coach came out and moved me to the mound. We were up by two and Eric was tired. I warmed up. We played six innings.

I saw him.

When did he get there?

Sitting right up on the top bleacher. Laughing and yucking it up with everyone. Everybody's friend. The whole town loved him. He made people laugh.

Not me. He never made me laugh.

Fuckin' asshole.

Fuckin' hypocrite.

Fuckin' drunk.

What's he gonna do? He's already wasted.

Maybe he'll pass out. He does that sometimes. Sometimes he even made it through the night.

Sometimes.

What's he gonna do?

I faced my first batter. Strike one. Ball. Ball two. Strike two. Ball three. Strike three. You're out!

The second batter popped out to the catcher.

Third batter.

Walk.

Batter number four. Bases loaded.

Strike one.

That'd be cool. I could strike him out. Then he'd never hurt me.

That would be good. No more hurting. No more tiger.

Strike two.

No more fuck'n tiger.

Smack!

Where'd it go? Someone's gonna catch it. Three outs! Someone's gotta catch it, right? Someone's gotta catch it…

No!

The ball landed between the outfielders in left center. Rolled all the way to the fuck'n fence.

The bases emptied.

I looked to the stands. He was gone.

The next batter came up and I struck him out on three pitches.

He was gone.

We came up to bat. Our last at bat. We needed one run.

One run.

But, he was gone…

Eric came up. Base hit.

Adrian came up. Base hit. Eric went to third.

I came up.

Strike one.

What am I gonna do? We could win. He might not be mad.

Ball one.

But he's already fuckin' wasted.

Ball two.

He's gonna kill me if we don't win. I don't know why, but he thinks I fuck up just to get him. Even if it's just something dumb like baseball.

I like baseball, though.

I love baseball.

I love pitching.

All alone.

Ball three.

If we don't win.

Strike two.

But, what if we win?

What if...

Whack! The ball left the bat. Eric bolted toward home.

Tying run.

I ran to first. Coach waved me on.

Adrian was breaking toward home.

The ball hit the fence.

The top of the fence.

It fell...

Out!

HOME RUN!!

We won!

He won't be mad now. He can't be mad now.

The whole team swarmed the plate and picked me up.

He has to be proud of me now, right?

Mom was at the game. We drove home, stopping at Jack-in-the-Box to pick up burgers.

"Sweetie, I am so proud of you! That was a great hit and you pitched so well," she said. "Makes me nervous some times when you pitch, but I am so proud of you!"

"Where'd he go?" I demanded. "He coulda seen us win. He coulda seen me hit a home run. Why'd he have to leave?"

I didn't really care that he'd left, I didn't want him there in the first place, but if he's coming he should at least stay for the end of the game.

She shivered a little. So's I wouldn't see her. But I did. I saw her. She was scared. "Honey, he just had some things to do and needed to go."

Yeah. "He couldn't even wait ten fuckin' minutes?" I almost never cussed in front of her, but I was mad.

Scared? And I was scared.

I was 11.

We got home with dinner. We went in and started to put the burgers on the table. She went into the living room to tell him about the ending of the game. How his son hit a home run.

He was wasted.

He was pissed.

"Home run! That little bastard gives up three runs to embarrass me and I have to leave with everyone looking at me! The fucker hit a home run!"

He came storming and stumbling into the kitchen, nearly taking the door off the hinges as he tried to catch himself.

"You get your skinny ass up stairs! I'll be there when I get there!" He cleared the table of everything with one sweep of his hand. "Be ready!"

"But...we won!" I said, trying to sound brave.

"Move! You little bastard, you embarrassed the shit outta me!"

"I hit a home run! They all cheered! All your friends cheered!"

"Now!"

I don't remember how many times he hit me.

Lost count...I bled on my bed.

But, we won!

We won the fuckin' game!

That Damn Belt!

Puberty...

I had hair.

Puberty.

I remember he laughed at me.

"Oh, the little boy has hair. You got balls now...does that make you a man? Do you think a few curlies make you a man? Gonna have sex now? No fuckin' way. No horny bitch'd have you!"

Puberty's supposed to be a good thing, right?

Growing up, right?

What's he mean, "*horny bitch*"?

Does he think he knows me?

Does he think he knows anything about me?

He has no idea that Ashelee even exists.

Don't know what he'd do if he did know.

The only clue he may have had was that he saw us walking home one day, a group of about ten of us. Ashelee and I loved to walk home with a few guys from the baseball team and a few cheerleaders...all of whom went to the church.

All of them tried to get me to go.

Though I knew she wanted me there, Ashelee never pushed. The others were not subtle, they all the time asked me to come to youth, to pray with them, to go to Bible study.

Sometimes I thought about it.

Asshole'd never let me go anyway. He wouldn't get anything out of it, so I couldn't do it.

One day we were walking home, singing and goofing off. Conner and I were the best pitcher/catcher battery the junior high had ever seen, or so they say, and the high school coach always had someone at our practices just to watch.

While Conner and I, goofing off and laughing, stumbled along, three things happened at the exact same second.

Conner grabbed my shirt, the sleeve ripped and he saw the fuck'n tiger. He gasped.

And, right at that second, my father came by, stopped and demanded that I get in.

"Hey Dan, get in the car, we need to get home. Hey kids, Dan's gotta get home today; has a few things that need to get taken care of."

Fuckin' hypocrite, putting on the face of such a kind and caring father. And me, the obedient loving son…yeah.

Still trying to adjust my shirt, I knew better than to respond, but something inside of me didn't care. "We were going over to Conner's house to study," I lied. We were planning on studying, but not at Conner's house, we were going to the church. They always studied there and had convinced me to go with them today. I wanted to go with them.

But no, not me…not today. That man shows up.

"Get in the car, now. We need to get home." The tone was one that to anyone else would sound normal, but I knew. Even though it was silent, even though no one heard it. I knew.

Only in his eyes, but I knew.

He exploded.

I swallowed hard… "I gotta get, guys. I'll see you tomorrow."

They all said their goodbyes. Ashelee gave me that look that she alone could give. A look of fear…fear for me. That was new. I never knew her to be scared for me before. But I could see it in her eyes.

Could she know?

We drove in silence and, as we pulled into the garage, he just looked at me and in menacingly quiet tones told me to "Get your fuckin' ass into the house and upstairs. You do not EVER tell me no. Particularly in front of your worthless friends!"

"I didn't say no. I only said we were going to study because we have test this week. You're all the time telling me to study, I was just trying to do what you wanted."

He slammed the door, grabbed my hand and threw me against the hood of the car. My face bounced off the hot metal, bruising my left eye. He said nothing, only laughed. Then he pulled me to him and, very quiet like, told me to get upstairs.

Asshole.

He made the number twenty-four then.

Every day.

I was a man now, he said. I needed more now, he said.
Much more.
Every fuckin' day.
I was 13.
That Damn Belt!

The Fight...

Don't mock Ashelee and, please, don't mock me.

No showers at Hinton Junior/Senior High. We could if we wanted after PE, but most of us never did.

Every fuck'n day I had to do a quick change in a stall, with my back to the john. Good thing no one had ever questioned it, cuz I don't know what I would do.

Today, though...

"Hey fag-boy! Whatcha scared of? No balls or no dick or are you ...a girl?"

Mark.

Why does he do this?

The door to the stall swung opened and there, in just his boxers, stood Mark. Tall, but not so big, just an ass always starting stuff with someone.

"Are you a girl? Fag-boy!"

"Fuck off, Mark, and leave me the hell alone!"

"Woo...big man uses big words. Girl's got no balls."

He pushed me. Fighting sucks, but he pushed me.

"Get the hell outta my face, Mark. You don't wanna go here, not now. Not today."

That look on his fuckin' face makes me laugh. He tries to play left field and he's good, but he thinks he's all that and now he wants to fight? What the fuckin hell is he doing?

"Watcha gonna do? Go crying to your whore, Gorshlee?"

That's it. No one says anything about Ashelee.

Ever.

"You don't EVER fuck'n talk like that about Ashelee. Ever. I'll kick your fuckin' ass all the way to hell." I threw Mark across the room and into the lockers.

They almost fell down. Wow, I thought, I didn't think they'd fall. They thundered all through the locker room. My arm was across his throat and he was choking.

"Danny," he gasped, "I can't breathe."

"You don't know anything the hell about me and you don't ever talk about her again," I growled, punching him in the gut over and over and over again. I hardly remember anything but being pissed and letting him know it. "Or about me. You have no balls and you have no guts and you're a pussy! I'll fuckin' kill you."

"Danny! Back off…" it was Conner. Conner was always in my corner, but here he is, sticking up for Mark. "Danny, you're gonna really hurt him. Back off, man, he's done."

Just then, I felt another hand on my back. "Daniel, let go." A voice boomed. "NOW!"

Coach Hawkins.

I let go.

Pussy boy dropped to the ground, gasping.

"Mark, get dressed and get out of here, NOW! You're lucky I came in. One of these days you will get yourself in some real trouble."

"'K coach, I will. Sorry, Dan…I'll see you at practice."

Coach got it.

"Danny, you need to breathe, buddy. I'll let this go today, but next time we'll have to suspend you."

"Okay, Coach…thanks."

I really think Coach got it. "Conner, stick with him until practice."

"Sure, Coach, no trouble."

I grabbed my bag. "Thanks, Conner. That fuckin' asshole shoulda died. Why does he do that?'

"I dunno, Danny, but… well. What the heck was that? I've never seen you do that before and Mark's always saying stuff."

"Nothin', Conner." That was a lie, but I couldn't tell him the truth. Right? "I've just had a shit day and he pushed my last fuckin' button."

"You've just been acting weird lately, man, and we're worried about you. Be careful, what if your dad heard?"

"Nothing, that man doesn't give much of a shit about anything but himself," I said, though I knew it would just give him another excuse to beat the shit outta me. "What did you mean by 'we,' when you said 'we're' worried about you'?"

He squeezed my shoulder. "Ash and I talk about you a ton. She loves you, you know. We pray for you and your family every time youth meets at church."

Prayer again? I forgot Conner did the whole youth group thing.

"Thanks, I guess." I breathed hard…sighing, really. "You two are my best friends, Conner, and I would kill if someone did something to Ashelee…or you. But something just snapped inside me. If kinda felt good."

It felt good?

That was the first time I thought that hitting someone could feel good. NO! NO! NO! NO!

It can't feel good…it can't! That would make me almost be able to understand that asshole.

We headed out toward the 200 building, math for Conner, History and Coach Hawkins for me. Ashelee had math with Conner. I liked high school, cuz I got to see Ashelee every day in every class but P.E. and Math.

"Dan?" Conner started.

"Yeah?" I said, not really hearing him.

As he turned toward his class, he looked at me and got my complete attention, "You 'member the other day, when we were walking home…well, what happened to your back? Do you need to talk about something? What was that thing?"

Fuck!

That Damn Belt!

Ashelee...

Pastors!
Churches!
Hypocrites!
Right?
Ashelee's dad?
Ashelee?
Never mind.

Ashelee always talked about church but she talked about it different than I'd ever heard it before.

"But, silly, it's your dad. You're suppose to say that, right?"

We were in the game room at her house and Ashe was telling me one more time again how cool church was and how easy her daddy is to talk to.

I remember the first time it came up, we'd been dating for about a week and she wouldn't kiss me. She wouldn't even let me kiss her cheek...nothing.

All the other kids I hung with were having blowjobs and hand jobs from their girlfriends. They said.

And giving their girlfriends handjobs and such. They said.

Most were having sex. They said.

But not us.

Nope.

"Why can't I kiss you? Do I smell? Am I really evil?"

"No, silly, you don't smell! Danny, you're great! It's just that kissing can lead to more stuff and I don't want to be tempted to go there. Ever!" she said it with a smile. "Until I'm married."

That sounded a whole bunch like a church thing to me. "That sounds like your dad talking," I told her. "I don't get it. What's the whole church thing about no sex, anyway?"

I'd known Ashelee pretty much all my life and, though we'd only been "together" for a few weeks now, I'd spent a ton of time with her when we were little. Her dad made the whole group of neighborhood kids a cool rock candy he says he invented. But, every time he was around, some how or another, God came up.

Still smiling, she continued, "Danny, God created sex. Do you believe that?"

"NO. You know I don't believe in God." I thought it over for a second, "But, if I did believe in God, I suppose it would make sense that He created sex. So, okay, God created sex. So what?"

"Well, if God created it, don't you think He'd know how to have the best sex? Don't you think He'd have the blue print for the best sex?"

"Yeah, okay. But, still, so what?"

"Well, silly, think about it. God tells us to wait until we're married. So, don't ya think that that's when it would be the best? Feel the greatest, last the longest?"

I had never thought of that. But there is no God or gods. How could there be? My father has to be proof that a God who loves us couldn't exist.

Right?

I mean, Ashelee's always talking about this Jesus guy…says He died for me and all. She doesn't preach, she just talks about Him like He's a real guy, or something.

Alive.

Right now.

I don't get it.

Her dad told me that too…he's a cool guy, for a pastor. He seems to understand things.

"You might be right, I suppose. I never thought about it like that, I never think much about the whole God thing, unless I'm with you. But I guess it makes sense."

She took my hand and just smiled at me. "I'm still praying for you, you know?" She said that a ton and, even though I refused to believe in her God, I think deep inside it made me feel good.

We'd been quiet for a few minutes after that when Ashelee suddenly changed the subject.

Huge.

It caught me by surprise.

"Danny," she said, "why did you ask if I thought you were really evil? Who says you're evil? Who woulda told you that? You don't really believe that, do you? Danny?"

There it was.

The question.

The evil.

I was stunned. She'd never asked me anything like that. No one had. If she didn't ask it, I would never have to answer. What do I say now?

"Danny?"

What do I say now? Why did she have to ask that? I suppose I could tell her anything.

I could lie. But, no, I'd never lied to Ashelee before. I couldn't start.

Why'd she have to ask me that?

That Damn Belt!

The Secret...

But she did ask.

Now what am I supposed to tell her? "Yeah duh, Sweetie. I have to be evil. Aren't we all...well, no. You aren't evil, but I know I am. I have to be. My father says I'm evil and he beats the shit outta me every single fuckin' day just to make sure I know it."

As I thought that through, Ash got right up close and looked at me right in my eyes.

Still, what do I say? I can't tell her. We'd been friends since we were three and I could never hide anything else from her, so what made me think I could hide this?

I can't tell her.

Not this!

Not ever!

Never!

Can I?

"Danny, talk to me. You know you can talk to me. Please!" She was whispering and holding my hands. "Please, Danny. I love you!"

I looked at her, and probably got that stupid grin on my face that I always seem to get. I get a shiver whenever she tells me that she loves me. I love her, too, I just don't say it very often.

Love scares me. I mean...my father loves me, too...right?

"Let's just go for a walk," I said.

That Damn Belt!

Out It Comes...

We went out and walked to the beach. I like walking by the lake 'cause it's the only place I can escape. I just have to make sure I'm home before he gets home, or he might...

I hate blood...especially my blood.

There's a spot. We like to call it 'our spot.'

As we headed outta her house, I took her hand and headed toward the end of the yard where the trail to the lake started.

Our Spot.

It's quiet.

It's far.

It's safe.

It's ours.

I can't tell her, she'll hate me. I love Ashelee so much. I don't think I could live without her.

Hmm...not living. I'd thought about that a lot lately.

There's that weird walking bridge thing up by the old salmon run...it'd be so easy, right? I could put a rope up there and slip it around my neck. No one would ever know. No one would ever care? Right? It'd be so simple...so easy...so over.

I'd be safe, right?

She was watching me. Her gaze penetrated me in a way that no one else's could. What could I do? What could I say?

She was quiet along the way. Just held my hand and looked into my soul.

There's an old tree that lies on the edge of the water where we can put our feet in and splash.

I like splashing Ashelee...she squeaks.

Not much squeaking tonight. We sat there and skipped pebbles across the water. Not much talking, just pebbles and ripples and...my friend, Ashelee.

Silence.

I could tell she was going to say something, but I didn't know what. I had a feeling, but I didn't know.

She had tears in her eyes. "Danny,,,what's going on? You seem agitated and almost mad…a lot." I'd never truly seen Ash cry. "All the time, Danny. Did I do something? Are you mad at me? Talk to me, Danny. Please!"

That Damn Belt!

"I'm not mad at you, Ash!" I sighed. "I don't think I've ever been mad at you. Why are you crying? Don't be sad."

"Danny, you said something about being evil." Real tears now. "Evil is horrible. Daddy told me that we are all born evil, but that doesn't mean in life we have to be evil. You don't do bad things. Everyone likes you…why would you think you're evil?"

I knew it. "You just said that your father told you everybody's evil."

Religion!

Ack! I knew it, judging and saying everybody's evil.

I got pissed. Not at her, but I was so pissed at life and people and…

That Damn Belt!

I looked away for a minute and then I did something I never did…ever.

"Did you just say that? I have to be evil…" Anger? I'd never snapped at Ash before. "Did you just say that? You said it!"

But she didn't get mad. "Danny, it's okay." She just looked at me. "Talk to me!"

"As
helee, I'm evil. I am. I've always been evil and I always will be. I don't even know why you like me so much!"

"Danny!"

Then something inside of me clicked.

Exploded, more, I suppose.

A valve opened and out it spilled.

Everything…tears, too.

That Damn Belt!

"He beats me, Ashelee!"

I said it. I didn't know why and I'm not real sure I even knew what I was doing, or why, but I had to tell someone and Ash is the only one I trust. I had to tell. I had to. It was almost as if I was pouring my guts all over the place. I don't know if I took a breath, but I was crying now, and spilling.

Everything!

"That man…I can't even call him my father…that man…he fuckin' beats my ass every single fuckin' day…every fuckin' day. I bleed, Ashelee. He fuckin' makes me bleed. He uses his belt. That Damn Belt! He uses the buckle of That Damn Belt and beats the living shit outta me. EVERY SINGLE FUCK'N DAY! He'll do it tonight, sure as we're sitting here. I hate him so much, Ashelee! It has a tiger head on it. The buckle has a fuckin' tiger head on it. He hits me with the fuckin' tiger head. You can see it on my back." I stood up, to take my shirt off, but didn't slow down. "You can see it on my ass…parts of that fuckin' tiger head all over the place."

I stopped to take a breath and pulled my shirt up. She stifled a gasp, but didn't say anything. I'd never taken my shirt off and, though she'd asked about it before, I always had an excuse.

"You're evil, he says. You're bad, he says. I'm in charge, he says. You need to know who the boss is, he says. You need to know whose house this is, he says. Who the fuckin' hell does he think I think is boss, Ashelee? What the hell? He fuckin' beats me every fuckin' night just to show me that I'm evil. Just to show me who's in charge. Who's the boss. Why does he have to do it? Why does he have to hit me? Why does he have to hate me? Why?"

She reached over to touch my back. Ashelee didn't hesitate, she just wanted to know.

"Why does he hate me, Ashelee? Why? What did I do? Every fuckin' night. Ever since I was three. The first time he didn't use the buckle, but I think he wanted to. Then one day, he made blood and he liked it."

I stood up again and undid my shorts. "Look at what that man did to me." She'd never seen me naked before and didn't now, but I showed her the top of my ass cuz I wanted her to see that tiger head. The whole head. "It's a tiger, Ashelee. A fuck'n tiger. He beats me with the fuck'n head of a tiger. I hurts so bad, Ashelee. It hurts s…." I was sobbing now.

It was out. I didn't even realize I was saying it. I just said it. I trust Ashelee more than anyone, but I didn't want her to know.

I never, ever, cried anymore.

Not in front of people.

Not in front of him.

And not in front of Ashelee.

I didn't think I even knew how to cry. I thought I'd forgotten.

Now what? What's she gonna do now? She's gonna leave. She's gonna up and walk outta my life. Then what? Now what? What did I do? Why did I tell her?

Death. I can't live without Ashelee. Maybe that'd be better, anyway.

Dying? No more pain, right?

Death can't be all bad?

Right?

She's gonna leave now.

That Damn Belt!

Now What...

But Ashelee didn't leave.

She just looked at me, tears streaming down her face...making a wet mark on her shirt. Then she reached over and pulled my shirt up to see my back again.

"Danny! Your back is so bad! You can see that horrible tiger all over your back. Even up here. Are they on your legs, too?"

I didn't tell her, but they were. All the way down the top of my legs. Not so bad as my back, but they were there.

I think she knew. Somehow I think she always knew.

Would she tell? Would she hate me?

Ashelee leaned across and just hugged me.

She didn't leave.

She stayed there and held me. No, I don't think she's gonna leave.

Not today.

Right now I just needed her to hold me.

She did.

Thank God.

"Why didn't you ever tell me, Danny? We've been friends for so long, maybe I coulda helped you."

"I'm all the time thinking that if I told you, you'd hate me. You'd know I was really evil and you'd hate me. I can't let you hate me, Ash. I can't!"

"Why would I hate you?"

I thought about that. I thought about who she really was. I thought about her father.

I thought about God.

Did I just thank God?

I don't even believe in Him.

Do I?

For what seemed like a million years, she didn't say a word, then, "I love you, Danny. I have always loved you. But, Danny, we need to tell Daddy. Daddy can help you, Danny."

There it was. Pastor Dad.

I knew it and I think it scared me most. She'd want to tell her father.

I don't think I meant to be loud. But...

"NO!" I screamed it. "We can't tell anyone. He'll kill me, Ash, he'll kill me. He beats me every night, Asheelee, and he'll do it tonight...like I said. If we tell, he'll kill me, Ashelee. He'll kill me, dead."

I was again thinking how bad being dead could possibly be. Better than this shit, that's for sure.

"Okay, Danny, okay. We won't tell him," she reassured me. "But, Daddy could help you. He likes you, Danny, and he prays for you. He prays for you all the time!"

That caught me. "He still prays for me? Why does he pray for me?" It's interesting, I suppose, how things start. "I don't even believe in God and your father's praying for me? Why?"

"You don't believe in God, Danny, but He believes in you."

Then she did something she'd never done. She kissed me. I always wanted to be the one who started that, but she kissed me. Right on the lips. "I pray for you, too, Danny. You know that." And then she held me.

Her too?

Yeah, I guess I knew that.

"Sometimes we pray together for you. All three of us, Mom, Dad and I, pray for you...every day. I won't tell him, Danny, I promise, but Daddy would be good to tell 'cause he knows how to help people."

"I hate him, Ash. I hate him so much! Why doesn't he love me? The man goes out and gets shit faced and it's my fault. Gets home from work late, it's my fault. Even if he has a great day; he still has to 'show' me."

I don't remember how long she held onto me, but it was a long time.

We both cried.

She prayed for me, "Jesus, please take care of Danny. I love him so much, Jesus, and so do You. Please take care of him. Protect him from his father. Change his father. Please, Jesus."

After a long time, we started walking again and this time we went for a longer walk than usual. Just strolling along by the water and talking and being quiet and walking and talking and being quiet. It was one of the best afternoons I ever had.

Ever.

Then it was time for me to go home. "I have to go, Ashelee. I don't wanna be in trouble...well, more trouble. Maybe today will be the day he doesn't do anything. Maybe."

"I'll keep praying for you, Danny, for sure. If you can, call me tonight. Late. Tell me what happens," she said, smiling. "I love you, Danny."

We walked to the end of the woods, hugged and Ashelee left to go home. She lives at the top of the hill by the big church. Her father's church.

Maybe today will be a good day. Maybe he won't hurt me.

Yeah, right!

That man…

Asshole!

I hate him!

That Damn Belt!

Nothing Ever Changes...

Why had I told her?

I dunno, but somehow it felt good. Sorta like I'd let go of something I was holding, or lifting, or carrying. Or...hiding.

Secrets suck!

I went home. Scared, but not so much. I'm glad I told her. I'm glad Ashelee knows. She needed to know. I needed someone to know. I needed her to know.

I got home. Mom was there. She said hi, with her typical "surface smile" that she always gave me. "How was your day, honey?" she asked.

"Good," I said. *Fat fuckin' lot you care*, I thought.

My mother could have said something. She coulda stopped him.

Couldn't she?

"I went for a walk, after, but all my homework's done."

"That's good. Go ahead and set up for dinner, your dad will be home soon," she said it almost like it was a good thing. "He's had a long day. Had to go in early and was going to stop off with some of his people on the way home."

Great! He's had a long day and he's stopping. That means he'll come home fuckin' shit-faced drunk.

Asshole!

Dinner was pretty good. Mom made some kinda turkey pasta stuff. I love pasta and that's one thing Mom does good—pasta.

My father didn't say too much, 'cept to give him his "damn beer." He didn't come in as blasted as I thought he would, but he had four beers with dinner and then took one with him to the TV den.

I was in my room. I'm always in my room.

Hiding?

No, not hiding exactly, but just safer to have distance.

Right?

It should be safer, but...

It was nearly 9:00 when the phone rang. It was Ash. She wanted to say hey and to tell me that her family had prayed for me tonight…special. She assured me that she hadn't told anyone, but wanted her mom and dad to know I needed a ton of prayer.

"Danny, things will change. I don't know how, but we prayed that God would touch your life and protect you and that Jesus would take care of you. The Bible says 'by His Stripes we are healed,' and that means that because He died for us…because He died for you, He will take care of us. He will take care of you!"

Slam!

I hadn't heard him coming.

Take care of me?

The door flew open. "What the fuck'n hell are you doing on the phone? I tried to make a call and the phone was tied up." He never uses the phone at home, he hates the phone. He was lying to me.

Again.

Duh, what else is new?

"Danny, what's that?"

"I gotta go, bye." I hung up on her. I hate that so much! She doesn't deserve that. I don't deserve her. She prayed for me…what can her God do for me?

What can any god do for me?

"Who was on the phone?"

"No one," I lied, but it was better than telling him about a girl.

"Who the hell was on the phone?" he screamed.

I didn't care anymore. He could hurt me, but he wasn't going to hurt Ashelee.

"No one!" I screamed back. "Someone had a math question and wanted to ask if I got it. I said no. End of story. It was no one!"

He got this look on his face where his whole face kinda twisted sideways. "Were you talking to your whore? Do you have a whore? Fuck no! No one would want your skinny, worthless ass."

He began to pull off his belt. "You know better than to lie to me! Get your clothes off…NOW!"

He hurt me so bad.

Made me spread my legs so the buckle'd hit my balls. They bleed, too, I suppose.

He hurt me so bad.

He made me count. He was so mad. I don't even know why, he just went off. I lost count at 31…

I don't remember anything after that. I woke up, still naked, at about 1:00 in the morning. I hurt so bad.

Tonight had been different.

God's gonna take care of me, huh? What the hell was that, then?

He hurt me so bad.

I went to the bathroom and took a shower. I had to get the blood off.

I had to?

What?

What did I have to do?

I think I knew, but I was scared.

He hurt me so bad.

I had to get out. I had to get out, soon. I had to get out... Now.

But, to where? Where do I go to hide from a man that the whole town likes? How do I hide from a man everyone admires? Where do I go in the middle of the night?

The woods?

Yeah, then what am I gonna do? Grizzly Danny? Yeah, like they wouldn't find me and then what?

The cops?

No! What're they gonna do?

My word against his...except...

But....he'd win. He always wins.

And then he'd beat me worse. Beat me harder. Beat me more.

What could be worse than tonight?

I didn't even want to think about that.

What then?

Where do I go? What do I do?

Death would be nice.

Right?

But, what if Ashelee's right?

If there is a God, then there is a hell. Wasn't I already in hell? If there was a real hell, I'm sure as shit gonna go there.

Not Ashelee, she's not gonna go there. She'd have a place in heaven, for sure. If there is a heaven... Right?

Would I miss her? Could I go with her?

If there is a God?

What then?

That Damn Belt!

Help Me...Please!

Ashelee.

Ashelee's house.

Ashelee's dad.

Could I go there?

No, it's 1:00 in the fuckin' morning. I can't go there.

Can I?

Yeah.

Ash said her father...her dad...could help. Wonder what it's like to have a dad. A real dad.

Maybe she was right.

Maybe.

Could I risk it?

What might happen?

Could it be worse than this?

Nothing is worse than this!

I didn't even get dressed; I just kept my sweats on, quietly slid the window up and jumped to the top of the car.

And then I ran.

Oh how I ran.

Faster than on the bases.

I ran.

Faster than in football.

I ran and ran.

Finally, I got to her house and...what?

What do I do now?

Ring the bell?

Throw a rock?

What do I do now?

I walked to the big tree under her window. I couldn't sit, not yet, it hurt so bad. I just stood there leaning against a split in the low branches, put my head in my hands and cried.

I cried.

What's gonna happen?

What if he wakes up?

What if he…no, he's probably passed out on the couch, same as always. Same as almost every fuckin' night.

I don't remember how long I stood there; I just remember crying harder than I'd ever cried before. I'd never run before. Oh yeah, I'd wanted to a few billion times, but never did.

I about jumped through the tree. A hand was on my shoulder.

Ashelee?

No, too big.

My father?

No, not big enough.

Slowly I looked up and saw him.

Ashelee's dad.

Smiling at me.

"Pastor Dad?"

"Hi Danny," he said, quietly. "I thought you might come by. I've been in my prayer closet all night, praying for you."

"Wha…what? What do you mean?"

"Ashelee told us that you needed special prayer tonight, so we prayed as a family for you…but, I think you already know that. Then, when she called and you hung up, I went into my little prayer closet and sought the Lord. I know you needed prayer tonight, though I'm not positive as to why, and the Lord let me know that you would be coming over. He's watching you, Danny. He loves you, Danny. Why don't you come in and let's chat. I'll put on some hot chocolate…Ash's waiting in the study."

What's gonna happen? What does he think?

Did he really know I was coming over?

How?

Is he gonna ask me questions?

Then what?

I was scared.

That Damn Belt!

Ashelee's Dad...

She was in her father's study, sitting on the couch, crying. She smiled at me, then got up and came over and held me.

Pastor Dad didn't seem like any father I knew. "Here's some coco, Danny, do you like marshmallows in yours?" He was so nice. So quiet.

What was he gonna say to me?

He motioned for us to have a seat.

It still hurt to sit, but I was so worn out I didn't care anymore. Besides, he was gonna let me sit next to Ashelee...on the couch.

He trusts me. He doesn't even know me, not really, and he trusts me.

"Danny, do you have something you need help with? How can I help you? Ashelee told me that you might need help, but she wouldn't say why."

Phew...I knew she wouldn't tell.

Not knowing really what I was supposed to do or even what I wanted to do, I just sat there for a few minutes, sweating and crying.

Confused.

"I...I'm not sure what to do," I stammered. "I'm kinda scared."

He was keeping his distance...across the room, but not behind his desk. "What are you scared of, Danny? Can you tell me? Do you know?"

Yeah, I did know. But, no, I can't tell...can I?

I was quiet for a very long time, sniffling mostly, but not saying anything. Finally, Ashelee looked at me, got on her knees and asked if I wanted to pray.

I couldn't speak, so I said nothing...I just nodded. I'd never asked for prayer, but for some reason, I wanted it now.

I'd heard her pray before, but this time was different. Pastor Dad and Ashelee both took my hands and then she started to talk...out loud...to no one...but, it was different than that. It was like she was really talking to Someone. Someone Whom she expected to answer.

"Hey Jesus, it's late and we're all tired, but we know You're here and we know You love us. Thanks, Jesus, for loving us. Thanks, Jesus, for loving Danny. Lord, we need You to help him now, Jesus. He needs You to help him now, Jesus. I know You can. I know You will. Help him, Jesus, to know You. Help him to know he can trust You Lord. Help him to know he can trust us. Thank You so much, Jesus, for hearing us and for answering us. We love You, Jesus."

Something was happening in me. I'm not real sure what, but something was different.

"Lord, thank You for calling us to come to You. Thank You, Father, for allowing us to come to the foot of Your cross and lay our burdens down."

"But bad things…sniff…sniff…happen all the time," I stammered.

"Father God," Pastor Dad continued, "You teach us that when we are in the valley, You will be there. You teach us that when we face troubles, You will lift us up on wings like the ones that an eagle has. Lord, show Danny that You are carrying him and that You love him. Lord, show me now how to help Danny. And, Lord, show Danny's father that You love him, too." I almost missed it. Why did he mention him? I suppose a pastor has to. Maybe if people prayed for that man, he'd stop.

Maybe.

But…now he was talking to me.

"Danny, tell me why you came over here tonight. What's going on?"

I'm not sure how I got going, but it spilled more than it had the first time, when I told Ashelee.

"He beats me! He fuckin'…oops, I'm sorry." I didn't want to cuss in front of Pastor Dad. "I mean, my stinkin' father beats me every night. With a belt. With the buckle on the belt…every night. He beats me every single night with the stink'n tiger on that stink'n belt buckle…until I bleed." I told him everything. I even told him about tonight. "Tonight he smacked my balls. He never hurt me as bad as tonight. He hurt me so bad, Pastor Dad. So bad!"

Then I sorta changed subjects. "How can Jesus love someone who sucks as much as me? If He does love me so much, why would He make my father beat me? I don't understand…all I want is for it to stop. He hurt me so bad!"

My whole body was shaking. Ashelee grabbed my arms and they were going so hard that she nearly fell. Pastor Dad came over and took a hold of my shoulders and hugged me, hard and long.

I'd never been hugged by a man before.

Never.

"All I want is for someone who loves me to take care of me. All I want is for him to stop hurting me. All I want is…" sniff…sniff. "Can your Jesus really help me, Ash? Really, truly help me? I don't know. I don't know. I just…please! Make it stop! Make him stop!" I'd been in there for half an hour and I hadn't stopped crying.

I think even Pastor Dad was crying by now. I knew Ashelee was. I felt like it was the first time anyone had truly cared about me. But, I was still scared. I'm not sure why, but tonight had been bad. Real bad.

"Danny, can you show my dad?" Ashelee asked. "Show him your back, Danny."

I looked at Pastor Dad, tentatively. Before today, I'd never shown anyone, not my whole back. Not that stupid tiger. I was scared, but I was noticing a change in me that I didn't really get.

"It's okay, Danny. You can show me anything you feel comfortable with. If you're scared, you don't have to."

I looked at Ashelee. "I'll go get some more coco and I'll be right back." Turning around, she quietly left the study.

I looked at Pastor Dad and began to shake again. I think I was getting mad. "Look what that asshole…sorry, look what that man did to me."

I pulled off my shirt and then I took my pants and boxers down and turned around. "It's a tiger. Every day. Every single fuckin' day…sorry." Pastor Dad put his hand on my shoulder as I pulled my pants back up.

"We're gonna help you, Danny. I promise."

Just then Ashelee walked back in, followed by her mother, carrying hot coco and cookies.

"How can you help me? No one can help me. He'll kill me if he knew I'd said anything. Everyone thinks he's this perfect man and all. He's a fuckin' asshole, he hates me and I don't know wh…" I collapsed to the floor and just started to sob.

Again.

Seemed like I was crying a ton.

I was.

"Help me, please!" I begged.

I just want it to be over.

Mrs. Pastor came over and surrounded me with her arms. She sat right down on the floor, right there with me and gave me the greatest hug I have ever had. She didn't say too much, just held me.

"Danny, we're gonna help you." Pastor Dad told me. "I promise."

How? was all I could think but, "Thank you," was what came out of my mouth.

"Why don't you stay here tonight, Danny?" Mrs. Pastor said. "You could use the guest room. It's private and quiet and you'll be safe there."

A night away.

Wow!

They wanted me to stay.

Yes!

No!

I couldn't stay. What would happen in the morning? What would that asshole do if he got up and I wasn't there?

I couldn't imagine.

I didn't want to imagine.

"No," I said, "it'd be worse if I don't go home." I wanted to stay so much. It was safe here. It was finally safe. They knew. But...if only.

"You call me first thing in the morning, Danny, no matter what," Pastor Dad said. "I don't want you to go home, but if you really think that's best, you call me first thing. Okay?"

It wasn't best, but it was the only way. "Okay."

That Damn Belt!

The Long Walk Home...

Pastor Dad.

He said he could help.

I couldn't understand how, not without making it worse. How do you put out a fire by throwing stuff at it? Did I throw stuff at it? Can Pastor Dad put it out? He wouldn't tell that man...asshole...would he? He wouldn't go to my house, would he?

Four o'clock...almost three hours later, I finally left Ashelee's house. I took the long way home...up through the woods and down the path by the river...near the swing. I had a lot of thinking to do. Ashelee's whole family had prayed for me. They had held me. They loved me.

Is that what love is? I'd never felt that way.

They loved me.

Is that how love feels?

They truly loved me.

I had come to the river and begun to follow the path that led down to the pond and the swing.

Maybe there was something to that whole "Jesus thing." Maybe. I dunno.

Ashelee seemed to know God would hear her. Pastor Dad and Mrs. Pastor seemed to know that God would hear them. They all seemed to know that God would answer them.

As I rounded the bend, I saw the swing hanging there unused by me for nearly a lifetime. Memories.

I felt mysteriously compelled to hold the swing in my hand. No idea why, but I had to touch it.

As I reached for the swing and ran my hands up and down along its rough edges, I felt its rough edges cut into my hands.

I felt something on my face.

Tears?

Tears.

I was crying.

Again.

Still?

The tears had begun to stream down my face and, as I let the swing go, I sat down by the river's edge and began to talk.

"Um...hey, Jesus," I said, in an almost silent whisper. "I don't get You. I don't understand how You could let that asshole fuckin' beat me. Why do you do that, Jesus? I just don't get it."

I was praying. Sort of.

I remembered something that Ash had said once, before she even knew anything. "Danny, Jesus loves you," she'd said. "Danny, bad stuff happens, but Jesus doesn't do it to us, people do it to us, or we do it to ourselves. Jesus just wants to be there with you to walk through life with you and to help you out. He loves you so, so much, Danny."

Okay, so if He loves me and He wants to help me, what do I do?

I remembered once, a long time ago, just sitting listening to Pastor Dad say stuff that I'd never believed before and some stuff that I'd never heard before. Stuff that I didn't understand. He never preached at me, he just told me stuff he knew was true.

"Danny," he'd begun, "Jesus loves you so much. I'm not sure what's happening in your life right now, but He wants to help you. He wants to take care of you, Danny, and the great part is that all you have to do is to ask Him."

I remembered, too, tonight as we were sitting on the couch, Ashelee took my hand out of her hand and she grabbed my face. "Danny, Jesus loves you so much...let Him in, please. He'll hold you and walk with you and smile at you and, Danny, He'll never...ever...hurt you. I promise!"

I don't know how long I sat there, but I was crying yet again. This time, though, it was weird.

Before I left, Pastor Dad had prayed again. "Father God," he'd said, "Lord, please take hold of Danny and show him Who You are. Lord, make Yourself real to Danny, come alive in him and, Lord, heal Danny, by the power of Your blood. And, Lord, with all that is going on in Danny's heart and life...heal him and walk with him through this fire. And, Lord, please help Danny to forgive his father."

That part I really didn't understand. Forgive?! Yeah.

He told me that I needed to forgive that man. I just looked at him and said, "I'm supposed to forgive him? How can I forget this?"

Then he said something that struck deep, something that stuck. "Danny, you're never going to forget because every time you take a shower, you will see the marks. But, Danny, the Bible says that if we forgive, then God will take it away from us. See, Danny, if you forgive your father then the Lord will take the burden away from you and it will become His problem. And, it will be your father's problem. But, it will NOT be yours anymore."

I looked down and found a rock in my hand. I threw it across the water. "I hate him, Jesus! I hate him so much! I can't take it anymore, Jesus, if You're there, please, please help me!"

Uh oh, I was praying again.

And crying.

Ashelee'd said it to me so many, many times. "Danny, He loves you so much!"

The rock skipped across the pond and the circles became larger and larger.

Like my problems.

Like...

That Damn Belt!

This Is My Time…

I sat and meditated on the ripples. On the circles. On my life, shit though it was.

As the ripples faded, I lay down and stared into the night—or early morning—sky.

I lay there looking up at the stars. On nights like that, cloudless with about a gazillion stars, I loved looking up into the black nothingness…a nothingness dotted with small pinpricks of light. It made me dream of going far, far away, to a safe place.

A place where love is.

A place where pain is not.

Can such a place exist? I found myself wondering that often, and wandering in my mind to places beyond the stars. Beyond pain.

I lay there thinking through my life. Through the things that Ashelee had always said. Through the things that Pastor Dad had said.

Hmm…I thought. A place where love is…a place where pain is not.

I wonder what it would be like to be beyond the stars. I could look down on things and be safe. No one could hurt me. No one could find me. I just wanted to be safe. Just wanted to be loved.

Someone would love me, right?

Right?

It finally began to hit me… It's my decision.

This was my time.

A place with no pain.

Someone Who truly loved me.

"Jesus…if You're really there and really love me…please help me. Come into my heart like Ashelee said. Help me…please…please…" I didn't know what to say, for sure, but I was talking. "I don't know what to say, Jesus, but I think I need to ask something about Your forgiving me. Pastor Dad says I should forgive my father…how do I do that? Can You forgive me, Jesus?"

I lay there, the stars as bright as I'd ever seen them, and I was talking to God. I'm not sure why. I'm not sure what made me believe, but suddenly, I did.

"Hey, Jesus, Ashelee and Pastor Dad…their whole family…they say You can help me and that You will if I ask. Jesus, please make him stop. Make that man stop hurting me. Please. All I want is for him to love me. All I want is for You to love me. Please, Jesus, won't You please love me?"

That Damn Belt!

One Last Time…

Renewed fear.

As I approached the house, I could tell that someone was awake. Who could be up?

Why?

No one ever climbed outta bed before I left for school and, well, my watch said 5:38.

Five-thirty eight and the lights downstairs were on.

The front door was locked. The back door should be locked.

I hadn't thought through getting back in…I had only wanted to escape.

Fuck!

What am I gonna do now?

The bathroom window.

Perfect!

No lock. I went to the side of the house facing town and tried to climb up…needed to reach the ledge, but I missed. Musta looked like some kinda fool, but I finally managed to set my foot on the baseboard of the house, about an inch wide, and pushed myself up to the window.

The window was open wider than usual. No surprise. In muggy weather my mother usually left windows open. I pulled myself up and through…landing on the top of the toilet with little more than a small thud. I jumped up and began to go to my room.

"Get your skinny white ass the fuck down here! Now!" He was up. He was drunk or hung over or both and he was pissed.

I walked into the kitchen to find the asshole, whose worthless sperm led to my shit-faced existence, sitting in his little bitty disgusting tighty-whities, coffee in hand, belt in lap.

"Where the fuck you been? What the hell you think you're doing, sneaking out of here? Out of my house, in the middle of the night?" He was screaming again and the look of rage in his eyes scared me. Asshole was dangerous…half naked and dangerous. Looking almost funny sitting there with his huge fat beer-belly hanging over his tighty-whities.

I felt sick.

I tried to remember that Pastor Dad knew everything now. I tried to believe it would be alright.

"You fuck'n horny little prick! I asked you a question…where the hell have you been?"

I tried to believe it would be alright.

They said that Jesus would help me, right?

I could believe that, right?

I wanted to believe. I wanted to believe that today would be different and that he wouldn't hurt me.

I was wrong.

He'd gotten up outta his chair and towered over me. Naked and smelling like a gross mixture of old beer and new b.o. I hated him so much. "You have one second to answer me!"

"I woke up and went for a walk."

Smack!

The hand caught me across the face.

This was new.

I don't think he'd ever actually hit me with his hand, always That Damn Belt, and never in the face.

"Don't you lie to me, you fuckin' sack of horse shit!" Smack!

This time I jumped back just enough to make the full force miss, but the tip of his wedding ring somehow connected with my cheek.

Wedding ring!

What a joke that was!

Blood.

I couldn't tell whether it was blood or a tear. Did it really matter?

No.

Why would he call me that? What would he do this time?

I'm his kid, right?

I'm his son.

Right?

"Get your little ass over here, get your clothes off and bend over the table. Now!"

I didn't know what else to do. It was almost like I was programmed to obey.

That Damn Belt!

Facing the Man...

He made me almost straddle the chair, forcing my legs apart. Again with the balls. Again with the blood.

I don't know why he was up so early. I don't know anything.

He was so drunk last night. Why isn't he hung over?

He never gets up before I'm gone for school, I don't remember ever seeing him in the morning before that day.

I thought... I don't know what I thought. Maybe something would be different.

I'd had the balls to run.

I'd had the balls to go to Ashelee's house.

Smack!

I sucked in a mouthful of air.

Smack!

I don't know how many smacks it took.

Something inside of me snapped.

Something inside of me changed.

Then I decided. Right then and right there. It was my time and this was the last time That Damn Belt was gonna hurt me.

Ever!

I remember standing up and spinning around to face him...

Right in his face.

I don't remember ever being that close.

So close I could taste his breath.

I screamed at him.

I yelled louder than I ever yelled before and it was rage and it wasn't a child's yell, it was the yell of a man. A man in pain. It came from desperation. A yell of anguish. It came, finally, to his face.

I was done.

"You fuckin' man! You asshole! You fucked my mother just to get yourself off and, sucks to be you, she got pregnant and, voila, you had me. You're my fuckin' father. You beat the living shit outta me every fuckin' day.

Well, that ends now. Right now! I found out tonight that there are people who love me. I found out tonight that I don't have to take this shit from you anymore. Not ever! You keep your fuckin' hands away from me! I'm tired of bleeding. I'm tired of crying. I'm tired of being scared. I know there is a God in heaven now. I know that He loves me. I know He sent His Son for me and I know that I am going to heaven. This town thinks you're all fuckin that, but you're not. You're just a pretty much worthless asshole who gets off on beating his kid."

I had no idea, then, where the strength or the bravery or the balls came from, but I wasn't finished and he wasn't moving. I still had my sweats around my ankles, but I pulled them up and got even closer to his face.

"I'm not a worthless piece of shit and you wanna know the hell of it? Neither are you." Couldn't believe I'd said that last part, but there it was and I continued. "I guess Christ loves you, too. The Bible says He does. He says He does.

"I do have a girlfriend. She is not a whore. I've never had sex with her and she will probably end up being my wife…Wow! Grandchildren! Like you'll ever get to see them. You will never touch me again!" Tears were pouring now, but I was regaining control of my emotions.

"The Bible says someplace that I am supposed to forgive you and I … I—" I could hardly get the words out. "I want to, I just don't know how. I do know, though, that you will stay the h…you will stay away from me." For some reason I couldn't cuss and I don't believe a cuss word crossed my lips after that morning.

He was looking at me with a stupid, blank, drunken almost dead stare, not believing what had happened. And, plainly, not knowing what to do.

It was finished.

The chimes in the living room clock struck 6:00 and a noise came from outside the back door.

Knocking?

Who would be knocking now?

At this hour?

He regained his thoughts and stared at me, the rage returning.

The knocking persisted. I went to the door, not so much scared as nervous and unsure of what would happen.

Pastor Dad!

"Hi, Danny! I thought I'd come by this morning and see if you wanted to come to the men's prayer meeting before school." He winked at me, knowing. I think that his timing could not have been better.

My father, embarrassed, I think by his state of undress, excused himself to put on some pants.

God to the rescue?

I didn't know, but I said sure and headed up to the shower.

My father bumped me as he came back in the kitchen to face Pastor Dad. "Mornin', Pastor. Nice to see you this morning. What're you preaching on this week? Has the flock kept you busy?" Though I was out of the room and Pastor Dad related the conversation to me later, I believe he said it with a wink. My father didn't believe in God and he'd never set foot in a church. "You are out kind of early this fine morning."

"Well, I know that many of Danny's friends come to the prayer breakfast and I thought it would be nice if Danny would join us. You're welcome to come as well, if you'd like to." I had walked in just in time to hear that, and I blanched. NO! I screamed to myself, but I don't know what scared me then. My father would never, ever enter a church. Ever.

"No, Pastor, I think I'll just shower and get ready for another work day."

Pastor Dad hadn't asked for permission to take me and I believe now that he would not have left that house without me. Not on that day.

My back ached.

My legs ached.

My butt ached.

My balls stung.

My face stung.

But, my heart was leaping as I walked out the door with Pastor Dad that morning. He gently put his arm on my shoulder as we headed down the walk and told me he loved me and had been praying for me since I'd left.

I turned and this time I did it.

I hugged him and I just held on. And cried.

I think he was crying, too. I think he knew what had happened and I think he knew something had changed me.

"Jesus doesn't lie, Danny. He says He'll walk with you for always and that He'll never, ever leave you or let you down. You know that, now, don't you?"

After a minute or two, we walked to the car and, when I looked in the back seat, I just started to laugh.

Ashelee!

I love her so much!

She got out and ran over. Grabbed me and held me.

I didn't even notice the pain that her hug sent radiating though my body as she grabbed my striped back.

She looked at me carefully. "Danny, your eye? What happened to your eye? Did he hit your eye? Danny?"

"Yeah,, he was mad that I'd been out all night...that I'd dared to leave. I told him I had just gone for a walk. He didn't believe me, he just swung his hand and caught my eye with his ring." I was sitting in the back seat feeling like I'd never felt before.

We went to the Bible Study and prayer breakfast. It was interesting. Kids were there who I didn't even know went to church. We talked about God. We talked about answer to prayer.

Pastor Dad prayed for me. He prayed so that no one, except the three of us, could tell he was talking about me. Or that man. I thought it was kinda cool the way he could do that.

I wondered if Jesus really heard him. I remember thinking that I hoped Jesus would hear him and that I hoped Jesus cared.

He did.

After the prayer meeting, which went on for about ninety minutes, I thanked Pastor Dad and Ashelee...for picking me up. "This was cool! I never heard that many people pray before. Thanks for taking me."

I paused for a minute, "Pastor Dad?"

"What's up, Danny?"

"Thanks for helping me. I never thought anyone could, 'cause I thought I was evil and that he was doing what he was supposed to do...you know, to evil people."

"Danny, we're all born evil, but the Lord loves each one of us. Even your father," he said. "But, He does NOT want parents hurting their children...His children. He does NOT want anyone hurting His children. What's been going on in your house is wrong and you are not evil, at least not anymore than any one of us."

Ashelee took my hand and, smiling the biggest smile ever, "See, Danny, I told you that you weren't evil."

I didn't remember the last time I'd truly smiled, but I smiled back at her. "Yeah, I remember." I did love Ashelee and was thinking about her and how happy it made me to be near her.

In the back of my mind, though, I was thinking about something else, something not too distant and still scary. I was confused about what was gonna happen next. I did have to go to school, after all, and then I would have to go home.

Right?

Home is the place where, when you go there, they have to let you in. I had heard that line in freshman English class. I think it came from a Robert Frost poem… "Mending Wall," wasn't it? But, did they really have to let me in? Yeah, I suppose, but then what?

Did I even want to go home?

No.

About that time, I noticed that Pastor Dad had taken a weird route to school. He had made a weird turn, a turn toward town.

"Where're we going?" I didn't say it out loud, but I was thinking it. Where were we going?

He slowed down in front of the big court building, the one where the judges were, and the lawyers, and the social workers, and…the cops.

What was he doing? Did he want me to tell someone else? What then? Jail for me? Jail for that man?

Or, help?

That Damn Belt!

The Cops...

I froze.

I think Ashelee could feel the fear, because my hands flinched and I gasped out loud.

"I have a friend who I'd like you to meet," Pastor Dad began. "He's an elder at church and plays lead guitar in our praise band. He's a detective and his name's Grayson and, Danny; he works with kids all the time. He teaches junior church and the kids love him. He's a good man, Danny. You'll like him. And, he'll definitely like you. Don't be scared, just trust." I don't know how he knew, but Ashelee's dad always seemed to know and, more than that, he understood.

"Ooo...kay," I responded, "but what do I have to say to him? Do I have to tell him everything that man did...does...to me?"

As we pulled to a stop, he reached around and put his hand on mine. "Danny, you can tell him as much or as little as you want to. As you feel you need to. And, Danny, you can trust this man."

"Daddy, can we pray?" Ashelee asked.

Pastor Dad got that huge grin on his face that always seemed to be right there. "That would be an outstanding idea, sweetheart. Let's pray."

He kept his hand on mine and took Ash's in his other hand. "Father God, we thank You first, for taking care of us. We thank You first for sending Your Son, Jesus the Christ, to die for each of us. Thank You, Lord! We thank You, Jesus, for going always before us and taking care of our smallest needs and, this morning, Lord, we thank You for going into Grayson's office ahead of us. Thank You, Jesus, for holding on to Danny this morning. Jesus, please give us each a peace that comes from knowing You are with us. Jesus, please give Danny a peace and a strength that comes directly from You, and Jesus, hold Danny. Lord, too, please give Grayson wisdom and direction as You take us to him for help. Finally, Lord, show Danny's father Who You are. Thank You, Lord, in the precious Name of Jesus Christ, our Lord and Savior. Amen."

"Amen," I said.

Detective Grayson, an enormously tall man with a massive smile on his face, stood up as we entered his office. Coming around the desk, he hugged Pastor Dad, gave Ashelee a high-five and shook my hand with vice grip-like force. He had a baseball cap on and, I noticed a trophy case behind his desk, which held, among other things, a Tony Gwynn bat and a Johnny Bench autographed picture. I liked the man immediately.

"Morning, y'all! What's new in the life of my favorite family?" Turns out Grayson's wife and two children had been killed in a traffic accident ten years ago.

"We're great, Gray!" Pastor Dad replied. "Prayer was a blessing this morning, and we had two visitors."

"So, what brings y'all fine folks downtown on this beautiful morning?"

Here we go. What am I supposed to tell him? Should I just skip it all and show him my back?

"Grayson, Danny has a few concerns about his relationship with his father and, while not wanting him to go to prison, he does want to have the situation rectified and for his father to get help." I liked the way Pastor Dad put things. Made them seem not so bad.

I found out later that Pastor Dad had wanted to front load Grayson, so they'd talked over coffee a few days ago. Then Pastor Dad had only his suspicions, but he knew that things would be coming to a head, soon.

"Well, Danny, what can I do for you? Does your father need help of some kind?" Grayson said, "Or do you?"

My father.

I hated that he was my father.

I hated that I couldn't bring myself to call him "Dad."

I hated that I needed help.

"He … that man…he drinks. He gets mad." I hesitated, "*really mad.*"

How much do I say?

Ashelee, who had been standing behind me, came around and kissed me square on the lips.

Right there.

Right in front of her father.

Right in front of a cop.

"Danny, I need to get a soda. Do you want one? I'll bring you a Coke, okay? Danny, show him your back. All of it. Just do it, Danny, and trust him. Please." And she kissed me again and headed out the door.

I looked at Pastor Dad, with a question on my face, he put his hand on my shoulder. "She's right, Danny, you can trust him. You can show him."

I sat there for what seemed like ever. Then, slowly, I forced myself to my feet and, beginning to shake violently again, I took off my shirt and pulled down my pants. "He gets really mad sometimes."

Though Grayson rose and touched the scars on my back, neither of the men spoke as I pulled my clothes back on. "Really mad!"

Grayson didn't say anything for a few minutes and the expression on his face betrayed nothing of what he may have been thinking. Ashelee came in just then carrying four bottles of pop. She handed one to each of us.

"Danny, I want you to know that we are going to help you, but I need you to allow me to do what I need to do. Do you understand?" Grayson had a loving, but serious look on his face.

He cared.

I wasn't sure if I did understand and, while I wasn't scared, I wasn't sure whether I liked what it all meant. What was I gonna have to do?

"Danny," Pastor Dad was talking now, "do you believe that we're not going to let him hurt you anymore? Do you trust that we're going to help you?"

"Yes."

I did. I didn't know why I believed. I'm not entirely sure what made me really believe that anything was going to change.

But, for the first time, I believed it.

I did.

Ashe had my hand and squeezed it as I spoke, "I guess you can do what you have to do."

I thought for a minute, and then something struck me. "Does anyone have to know? Can we sorta keep it to ourselves…sorta?"

"We'll see what we can do, Danny," Grayson began, seriously. "It's going to be hard, at first, but we'll see what we can do."

That Damn Belt!

Fathers and Sons...

What's the relationship that fathers and sons are supposed to have? I'd had the opportunity to give that question a ton of thought and...I have no real example.

My father?

No!

The Bible says something about fathers loving their sons and being kind to them and training them up in the way they should go. How did my father train me up?

Strange things happen with pastors...lessons and thoughts come from odd places.

Pastor Dad, for example, had peculiar tastes in music. I found that many of his favorite artists, Neil Young and Cat Stevens, to name a few, seemed to know how I felt...sorta.

Maybe.

Cat Stevens seems like he knew me...like he'd been inside my soul. His song "Father and Son"...Wow! *All the times that I cried, keeping all the things I knew inside. It's hard, but it's harder to ignore it...*"

I hid the trouble.

I ran from the trouble.

Did I ignore the trouble? For a long time, yes. But now?

"*Ol' man, look at my life...*" Neil Young starts. "*I'm a lot like you were.*" What the hell is that? I'm not gonna be like him. I can't be like him. I'd rather die. "*Love lost, such a cost. Give me things that don't get lost.*" What does he mean, love lost? You gotta have it to lose it, right?

I think, often, about what it would be like to be a father. To be a dad. I want to have children, but...what if? What if I turn out just like him?

Like it says in that one song...I forget who sings it...about cradles and cats and fathers and sons turning out to be each other and the same. If I turn out like him...

Could I ever treat a child like he treats me? It's not normal, right? I know that now...finally.

Finally.

If I turn out like him, that would be bad. Fathers need to love their sons. Pastor Dad says that being a father is a physical action that takes one second's total time, but being a dad is a commitment that lasts forever.

How true is that? I dream that I can have a family like that.

Neil Young does say, though, that "*I need someone to love me...*"

Ya think! I've only ever really felt like Ashelee loved me...until now.

Until Jesus.

Until Pastor Dad.

Until now.

Never!

That Damn Belt!

The End...the Beginning...Living Forever

I still remember that belt, but the end came fourteen years ago, right before my 16th birthday. As I write this, approaching my 30th birthday, Ashelee and I have been married for eight years and are the parents of three beautiful children. Jon Ralph and Ashley Dawn are three-year-old twins, and Jessie just had her sixth birthday.

Much has changed in these last years. I went to college near my hometown and later finished seminary. I work with Pastor Dad now. Imagine that, a youth pastor! Makes me marvel daily at what the Lord can do and what He has done in my life and the distance He's brought me.

Pastor Dad and Mrs. Pastor (I guess I'll always call them that) were right. I forgave my father. Ashelee told me that once I'd forgiven him, God would take care of the rest and the anger would slowly go.

I did.

It did.

I changed.

I don't cuss anymore and I'm not scared anymore.

My father changed.

It took a long time, but he changed. Detective Grayson arrested him shortly after we left the police station and, instead of prison time, which I now believe would have killed him, they put him in a Christ-based psychiatric hospital where he got the help he needed.

There were reasons my father did the things he did to me and my mother. There was a source of the rage, but that's not the point here. The point is that the Lord healed my father and... He forgave my father.

My mother.

My mother married a man with such deeply seated and ingrained rage that, in reality, she never had a chance. I wish I'd known, maybe I would never have been angry with her. I blamed her for not helping me, but... I didn't know.

Mother didn't know Jesus, but she did know fear.

When he drank, my father beat her, not daily and not with a belt, but he did beat her. He would hit my mother for just about anything. One time she went to the hospital and it almost stopped then, but she lied to the doctors about her "accident," and they never did anything.

It didn't stop. I think he would have killed her if I didn't come along.

Turns out her pregnancy and my birth saved her life. He had a new target and it started early.

I am grieved, now, that I never truly had the opportunity to know my father as dad...or as a man of God. I prayed that he would come to know Jesus, but his drinking had so destroyed his liver that he died not too many months after our final confrontation.

He knew I had forgiven him and for that I am forever thankful.

We did speak one day and he did tell me that he was sorry and we cried together when he realized what forgiveness meant. I don't know if he ever met Jesus in this life, but I do know he heard the story.

That day will remain with me forever. When I went to see my father in the hospital, the cancer had taken him quickly. It had been about a year from the last time I'd seen him. The state hospital hadn't allowed visitors, until they determined he was truly physically sick.

"Dad?" It was the first time I ever called him that and, well, it wasn't really him. Tubes everywhere.

"Danny," he gasped, "I don't know how to say anything to you and I know you don't give a rip about me or what I say, but..." He had tears. "Pastor and his wife were here this morning, Danny. We talked for a long time. They said Jesus loves me and He died for even me. Danny, the shit I put you through, how can He forgive me? How can you? I love you, Danny. I'm so sorry. Please forgive me."

My father died that day and I never said anything to him. I was too angry, still. I knew I should. I wanted to, but I couldn't yet. I will always hope he knows now. I know that I'll see him in heaven and—with no tiger marks—I will give my dad a hug!

Ashelee and I delight in each other. There's no one on earth who I'd rather be around. We laugh, we play, we pray, we sing and we serve the Lord together. We even still go down to the river and she squeaks...only now the kids get a kick out of Mommy's giggles.

The Lord tells us in the book of Psalms to "Trust in the Lord and do good; dwell in the land and enjoy safe pasture. Delight yourself in the Lord and He will give you the desires of your heart. Commit your way to the Lord; trust in

Him and He will do this: He will make your righteousness shine like the dawn, the justice of your cause like the noonday sun. Be still before the Lord and wait patiently for Him; do not fret when men succeed in their ways, when they carry out their wicked schemes."

Never has this statement stood out more clearly than in my life and that of my family. I learned, after a time of hell on earth, to trust in the Lord and, as I began to do that, as I began to get to know Who He is, I began to delight in myself in Him. It was then that things truly began to change.

I am just at the beginning of an eternity serving the Lord, which will culminate in glorifying Him in Heaven. My wife loves Jesus. My children love Jesus. My mother met Jesus following my father's funeral and she loves Jesus.

I love Jesus. He took me in His arms and He has taken my past and allowed me to grow.

I no longer have fear for anything this world may offer...I no longer have fear of... that belt!

What About You?

The story you read, though not true is, nonetheless, very real. Danny, though not a real person, is a compilation of several young people I have known over the years. Danny waited for many years before he was able to share with anyone and, even then, it was very hard for him. Danny was afraid and Danny thought what his father did was normal. It was not normal. It was not right, and Danny needed help.

If you, or someone you know, is being hurt by someone—anyone—please tell an adult. Tell a coach, a teacher, a pastor or youth pastor. Tell the trusted parent of a friend. If you do not know an adult whom you can trust, please call the police. You are the victim. You do NOT deserve abuse, any kind of abuse. Ask for help, you do not have to live with the pain and the horror of someone who is hurting you.

Printed in the United States
68051LVS00003B/189